LONA

A Fairy Tale

Once upon a time, when magic was common and princesses were plentiful, there lived a powerful wizard named Druth. He could transform a prince into a toad or a shepherd boy into a sheep by a mere flick of his finger. But he could not—he simply could not—turn a princess into anything at all!

Enraged and humiliated, Druth took revenge upon three kingdoms whose princesses he could not enchant by imprisoning the people in a deep, unending sleep. He saved one lone princess, however, a baby named Lona, whom he planned to raise himself until she was old enough, and indeed worthy enough, to try to enchant. Some new spell, he was certain, would succeed. But when she grew up Lona showed surprising courage, and challenged the mighty wizard's power.

Through Dare Wright's superb language and unique photographs, readers will breathlessly follow each moment of Lona's remarkable struggle to remove the spell over the three kingdoms.

Especially enjoyable for reading aloud, LONA is an exquisite fairy tale. Its delicacy, wit and wisdom will deeply impress readers of all ages.

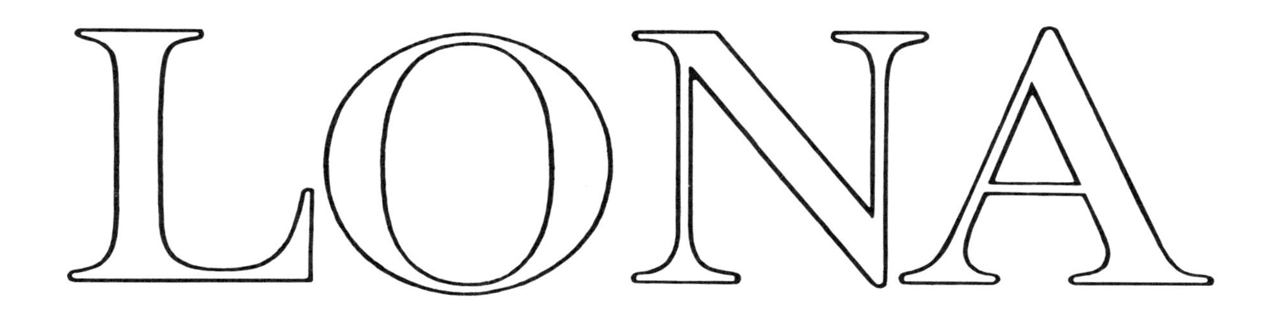

A Fairy Tale

DARE WRIGHT

RANDOM HOUSE • NEW YORK

—to my mother—

 Published in New York by Random House, Inc., and simultaneously in Toronto, Canada, by Random House of Canada, Limited. Manufactured in the United States of America. Library of Congress catalog card number: 63-7814

Once upon a time, when magic was common and princesses were plentiful, there were three kingdoms. In a valley ringed with mountains lay Muirlan of the green fields and quiet villages, Lasair with its deep forests and clear streams, and Yarmailt, where the sun was never too hot and all the rains were gentle. They were happy kingdoms. All their wars were done, and all their kings were wise. There was justice in the castles, and singing in the fields.

Only one thing troubled their peace. In a squat, dark tower on their borders dwelt a wicked wizard named Druth. Druth was a mighty wizard, and the people of the three kingdoms walked always in the shadow of his magic. He could summon wind, and fire, and water to do his bidding. He could turn a king into a black raven, or a shepherd boy into one of his own sheep. He could fashion maidens out of geese, and make fish leap from the sea and deer run toward the hunter's arrow.

But there was one thing Druth could not do. He could not change a princess into anything at all! It was long and long ago when he was a young and inexperienced wizard that Druth had lost his power over princesses. One day he had opened his huge book of common spells to the chapter headed "PRINCESSES: Enchantment of," and had begun to turn the princess of Muirlan into a little golden fish. Then he made a mistake. He got just one word of the spell wrong, and instead of the princess turning into a fish, all over the world fish who were really enchanted princesses regained their true forms. It did not matter that Druth had done a good deed quite by accident. The powers of evil punished his carelessness. Invisible hands ripped the whole chapter on princesses from the book, and every memory of it was erased from Druth's head. In all other wicked sorceries his knowledge increased with the years, but generation after generation of princesses grew up in the three kingdoms perfectly safe from any spell of Druth's. It was enough to humiliate any wizard.

Druth began to stay the year round in his tower, poring over his magic books. Sometimes his head dropped forward, and while he napped he dreamed of princesses, dozens of princesses, all turned by him into bats, or swans, or frogs, or snakes. For hundreds of years he had little time to bother the people of the three kingdoms. Then at last there came a day when he closed his books and smiled, and looked around for a princess.

Leaning out of her tower window was Aline of Muirlan, the great-great-great-granddaughter of his first failure. Upon her Druth cast his spell, the fruit of centuries of study.

Nothing happened!

A terrible temper shook Druth. He called on the waters, and drowned Muirlan deep under a lake, and made its people captive in an enchanted sleep. In the lake's green depths they slumbered helplessly.

Next Druth tried his spell upon the princess of Lasair. She was singing as she gathered flowers in the castle garden. Unchanged, she plucked another rose, and went right on singing.

Druth raged until the stones of his tower quivered. He sent wind and fire to burn the forests and dry up the streams of Lasair. Enthralled in a deep magic sleep the people sank down among the smouldering ruins of their homes.

Only one princess was left now in the three kingdoms, Lona of Yarmailt. She was just a baby princess, not quite steady on her feet yet, too young to be worth enchanting.

"She'll grow," thought Druth, and over Yarmailt he rolled a dense fog, imprisoning the land in blinding dampness, and its people in unending slumber. He stole the princess, and hid her away in a castle on a mountaintop. There he would keep her, available for enchanting, and by the time she was grown he would have a new spell ready.

Druth went back to his books.

Now the king of the drowned land of Muirlan had a son, Rogain, who had been off seeing the world beyond the mountains. Prince Rogain came home on the very day the fog spread over Yarmailt. He looked down from the mountaintops and saw a lake where Muirlan should have been, Lasair all scorched and black, and fog-enshrouded Yarmailt, where one great castle rose above the mist. He knew that only Druth the Wizard could have wrought such desolation!

No one ever ventured near Druth's dark tower, but Rogain's grief and anger drove him straight to its door. He beat upon it with his sword, crying, "Wretched magician, I am Rogain of Muirlan. Come out and face me."

Princes were no problem to Druth. Not even the magic jewel which Rogain wore about his neck—the jewel which had guarded every prince of Muirlan since time began—was proof against the wizard's power. Druth waved a finger and muttered a word, and in Rogain's place squatted a toad, lumpish and warty, with the great jewel of Muirlan gleaming in its head. The toad hurled its small body angrily against the door until Druth flung it open and shouted, "Begone, or you are a dead toad. The three kingdoms are destroyed, and they will stay destroyed. The Princess Lona is imprisoned, and imprisoned she'll remain until the day I enchant her." And the door slammed shut.

The toad who was Rogain hopped away, and as he hopped he thought. A toad could not wield a sword, nor do battle for a princess, but there were ways of outwitting wizards, and even a toad could learn.

"There are good spells as well as evil in the world," thought Rogain. "In the lands beyond the mountains I will seek a stronger magic than Druth's."

Rogain went first to the castle above the mist to see the little Lona. He was not used as yet to living in the body of a toad, and the rocky steps seemed steep and endless. He arrived quite out of breath, and the baby princess, not a bit frightened by his ugliness, laughed and patted him with her small, fat hands.

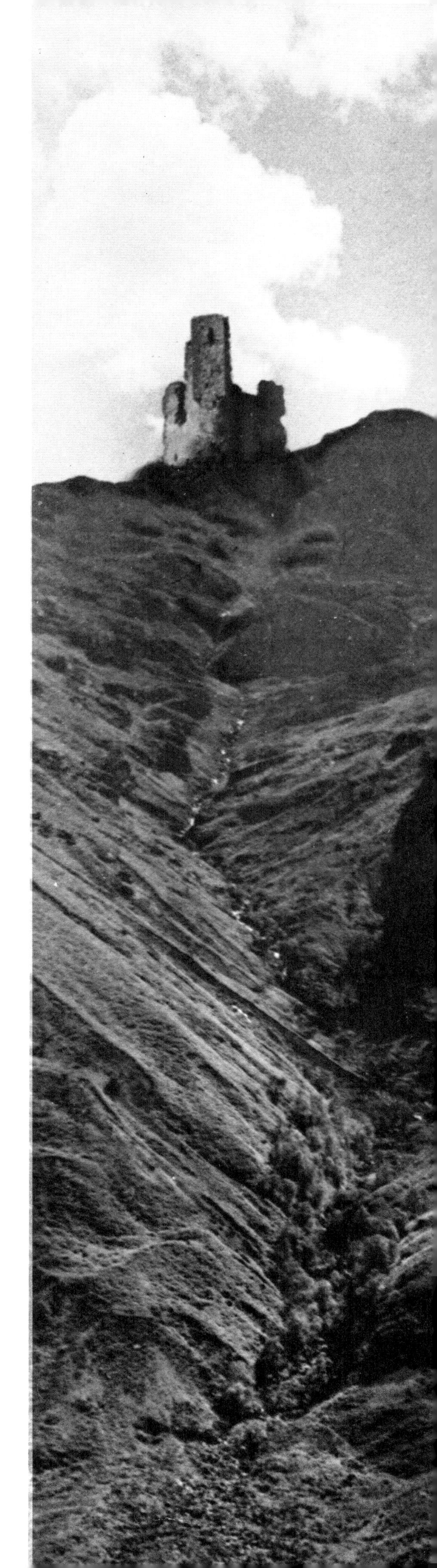

The years slipped by, and Rogain traveled all the winding ways of the world on his search. Among the wielders of good magic there was a legend, vague as smoke, of the spell cast over Druth long ago by the powers of darkness. But not a witch, a wizard, or a fairy could Rogain find to tell him of its terms. He followed rumors, and hopped after whispers, but every spring when the wind grew soft, and green began to mist the trees, he returned to Yarmailt to see the Princess Lona.

She was growing up alone in the tall castle. From year's end to year's end all she saw was the fog lapping at the battlements.

Invisible hands served her, but no voice ever spoke in the great stone halls. She had food, and clothes, and books, for Druth the Wizard had no wish to enchant a princess who was starving, or shabby, or ignorant. He wanted her beautiful and accomplished to make his triumph all the greater. Lona had every luxury, but no friend in all the world save Rogain the Toad.

Lona's heart always lifted when she heard the hop and the plop of Rogain's yearly coming on the stairs. Crying "Dear Toad, dear Rogain," she would run to meet him, and lift him in her slim hands, and drown him in questions about the world she had never seen.

Best of all, Lona loved to hear Rogain tell of the three kingdoms and their people. By the time she was five she could sing the little songs the mothers of Muirlan, and Lasair, and Yarmailt had always taught their children. By the time she was ten she could describe how the fields of Muirlan had looked on a spring morning, and what it was like to lie by a swift-flowing stream in Lasair with the green trees murmuring overhead, and just how fair a land Yarmailt had been. By the time she was fifteen she had learned of Druth and his enchantments. She wept so bitterly when Rogain told her of the fate of the kingdoms that he could never bear to grieve her with the story of his own enchantment. Toad he was, and a toad he let her believe him. By the time she was seventeen Rogain knew that he had come to love Lona truly, and that he desired her freedom even before the freedom of the three kingdoms.

But Lona, in the long months between Rogain's visits, dreamed of little else but rescuing the kingdoms. Whenever she stood in the window embrasures to look down on the floor of fog, she pictured a land lying fair in the sunlight, with smoke rising from the chimneys again, and travelers on the roads. Sitting alone over her embroidery in the torchlight, she imagined her silent castle filled with people, and Toad beside her every day of the year—for Lona loved Rogain as much as he loved her.

Lona was eighteen, and Druth was perfecting his latest spell, the spring that Rogain came to Yarmailt with the answer to his quest.

In a far corner of the world he had found at last an ancient witch who remembered the youth of the Wizard Druth and the spell he had provoked upon himself. The cave where she dwelt was hung with bats and dim with cobwebs, and the witch herself was small as any bat and frailer than the cobwebs, but her memory was long. Her thin, old voice wove the spell: "If ever Druth transforms a princess he himself will perish. But never can he transform a princess unless a princess herself permits it. Are the princesses brave nowadays, Rogain the Toad? It will take a brave princess to submit to Druth's enchanting. When the time comes she must call three times upon his name. He will change the princess as he chooses, not knowing he destroys himself. But first, one by one, the kingdoms must be freed. There is a magic shell to roll the waters back from Muirlan, a burning key to grow again the forests of Lasair, and a golden crown to banish fog forever from Yarmailt. The princess must go alone to find them. Give her the jewel from your head to guide her. And let her beware of giving in to fear. As long as she goes forward Druth cannot stay her, but each time she runs away from danger his power over her will grow. Should he enchant her too soon the kingdoms are lost forever. Do you know of a princess willing to sacrifice herself for the sake of others?"

"I know such a princess," said Rogain, "but I would rather die or stay a toad forever than have one hair of her head changed."

"The choice is hers, not yours. You asked, and cannot now undo the answer. You must tell her. Do not worry. She may refuse. People are seldom as brave as you expect," said the crone chuckling.

All the long road home Rogain grieved. With every hop his heart grew heavier. When Lona once again took him up in her hands, and lifted him so that he could look into her grey eyes, he sighed deeply and told her all that he had learned.

Lona only smiled and nodded.

"Refuse, I pray you!" cried Rogain. "I'll not have you changed to suit Druth's malicious fancy. You'll give him power to make you anything he chooses—even a toad as hideous as I am."

"But I would like to be like you," said Lona, who was too unworldly to value her beauty, "and does it matter what I become if only the kingdoms rise again?"

Thus Lona chose, and Rogain could not change her mind.

"Then take the only help I am allowed to give you," he told her. "Pull the jewel from my head to be your guide, and my heart goes with you."

Sadly, sadly Rogain hopped away.

Almost before the sound of his going had faded in the distance, Lona followed him down to where the steps vanished into the fog. Many a time she had stood in this archway, dabbling her toes in the tendrils of mist, and feeling little shivers of fright run up and down her back at the touch of the fog. Now she plunged boldly into the clammy, blinding wetness. Half-seen shapes clutched at her. Weird noises came and went—one moment whispering in her ear, the next sounding like the echoes of evil deeds done far away. Lona forgot Rogain's warning. She turned and ran in panic—back up the steps and through the courtyard—and the fog followed at her frightened heels.

Round and round the spiral stairs to her room in the topmost turret she stumbled.

She scrambled out of her clothes, and into the safety of her bed, and pulled the covers over her head like a terrified child.

Over the mountains in his gloomy tower Druth the Wizard was stirred by the wave of her fear.

"My spell is ready now," he cried aloud, "and the Princess Lona has grown tall and fair. Never was there a more enchantable princess. This will be my moment!"

He sent his spell winging straight toward the turret chamber above the fog, but, to his fury, nothing changed but Lona's size. She shrank and shrank, and when she stopped shivering and poked her head out from under the covers she was no bigger than a doll. Her bed stretched around her as wide as a meadow, and Lona imagined a whole world just as huge lying in wait beyond her room.

Could so small a princess save three kingdoms?

Lona still meant to try.

The long folds of her nightgown tripped her at every step. She could hardly pull its weight across the floor.

The drawers of her clothes chest seemed beyond her strength to budge. She tugged and tugged until at last her clothes were spilling out, but her dresses were as big as tents to Lona now, and she could hardly lift her shoes.

"It's all my own fault," mourned Lona. "If I hadn't run away Druth would never have had the power to make me small. Whatever shall I do? I can't set out without any clothes."

She sat on the floor in the flood of silks and satins and brocades, and wept for shame at failing her first test, then mopped her wet face on a lace-edged handkerchief. The handerchief reached all the way from her nose to her toes, and suddenly Lona thought, "Why I can make a dress out of handkerchiefs."

She cut, and sewed, and fitted until a small white dress took shape. The needle was as long in her hand as a dagger, and kept pricking her. Miniature drops of blood fell on her new dress. They were as red as the little scarlet cloak she fashioned from a piece of her best winter petticoat.

The setting sun was sending long shafts of golden light through the narrow window slits by the time that Lona was dressed and ready, with Toad's jewel held fast in her hand. She took a last look around the familiar room, and turned to open her door. The latch was high above her reach now! Inch by slow inch she dragged a heavy stool across the floor, and scrambled up on it. Standing on tiptoe she could just lift the latch.

Twilight had fallen now, and the steps which she had run up so fast not long before looked steep and dangerous. The cold stones were rough under her tiny, bare feet, for she had no shoes. They had been beyond her making. Fingers of fog clung to the stairs, and crept up to meet her. Lona shrank from their touch but she went on, clutching Rogain's jewel more tightly in her hand.

Druth in his tower crouched over a fire of herbs, watching Lona in its magic smoke and spinning spells to keep her in the castle. But he was as powerless as the witch had foretold. Only through her own fear could Druth stay Lona now.

Druth gnashed his teeth in rage. This princess was his property, raised just for his enchanting. It was intolerable that she should thwart him!

"Am I never to have any luck with princesses?" he groaned, "I'll not stand for this! Lona must stay secure in her own castle awaiting my next spell. If magic will no longer hold her there, I'll frighten her into turning back to the safety that she has always known. She'll never have the courage to pass the terrors that I can conjure up."

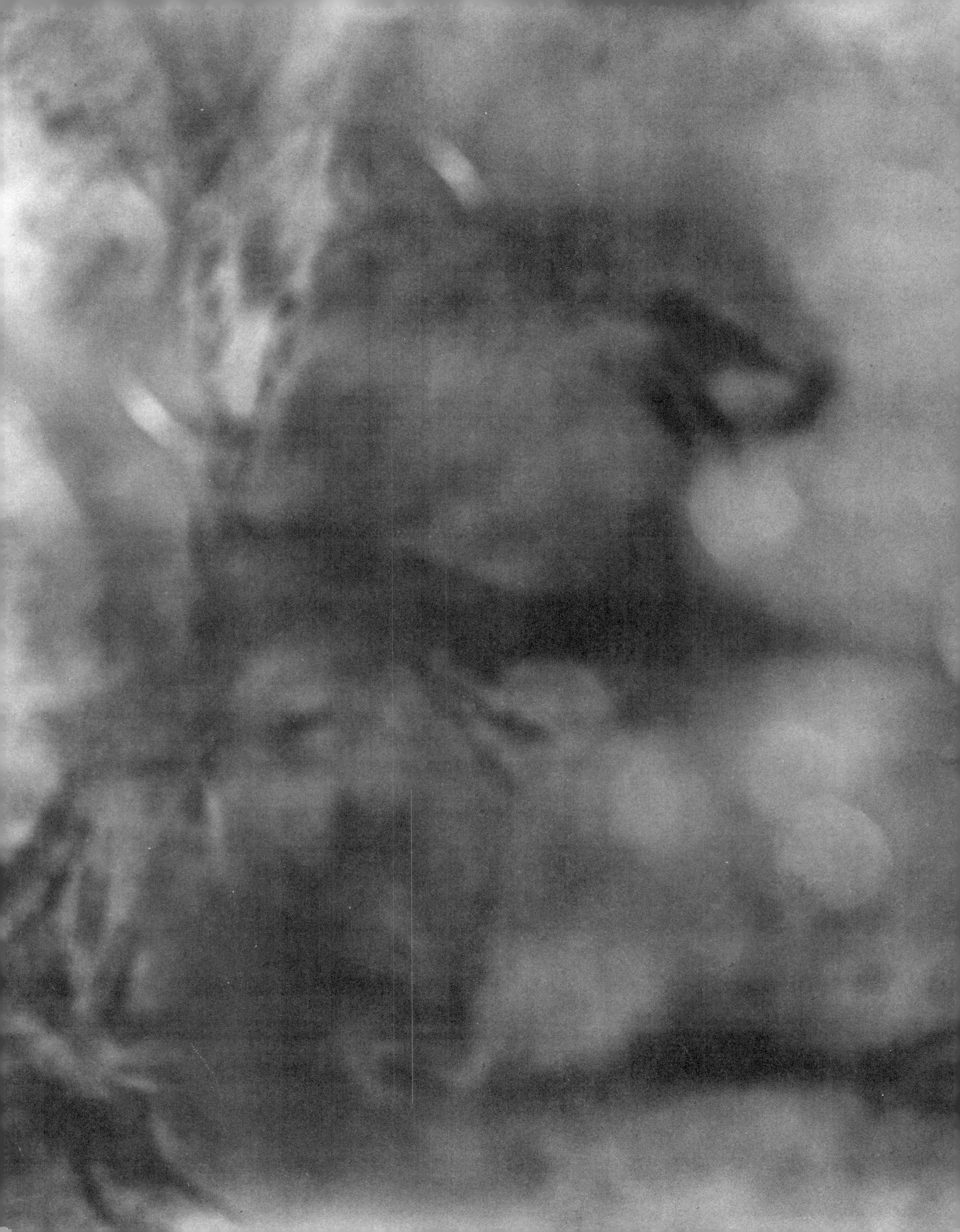

Across the darkening courtyard and down the outer steps Lona passed like a small shadow until she stood again in the archway above the fog. Her heart beat fast with fear but she went on.

Druth sat in his tower inventing evil apparitions to put in her way. Lona met things in the murk that crawled, and shapes that slithered, and beasts that flew. Sweet voices mocked her and led her astray into swamps which would have sucked her down into their slime had she weighed any more than a bird.

Lona no longer knew which way she had come, nor which way she was going. She was near to tears when still another voice spoke. But this voice came from the jewel in her hand and had a sound of Rogain's own.

"Hold me out before you," said the jewel, "and follow my gleam. If you stray from your path my light will dim. Turn back, and you will hold only a dull and silent stone."

Lona obeyed the voice. Her eyes were fixed so hard upon the jewel, and her ears were listening so eagerly to hear it speak again, that Druth's horrors went unnoticed now. Even time went unnoticed. In hours, or days, the fog grew thin and luminous, and Lona stumbled out into a narrow sunlit street.

The houses seemed to lean to look at her, but no faces showed at the windows, no footsteps sounded on the cobbles, no bustle of people crowded the doorways. This town just beyond enchanted Yarmailt had been abandoned long ago. Who would stay where wisps of Druth's evil fog eddied through the streets night and day? Lord and lady, burgher and peasant were all gone to live their lives where Druth was only a name to frighten their children.

This was Lona's first glimpse of the world beyond her castle. She stretched to peer into every window within reach, but there was only thick dust in the empty rooms. Even the mice had gone when the last crumb was eaten.

Lona slept curled on a doorstep like a kitten, and when dawn came the jewel led her silently out of the silent town, and into a wood as silent.

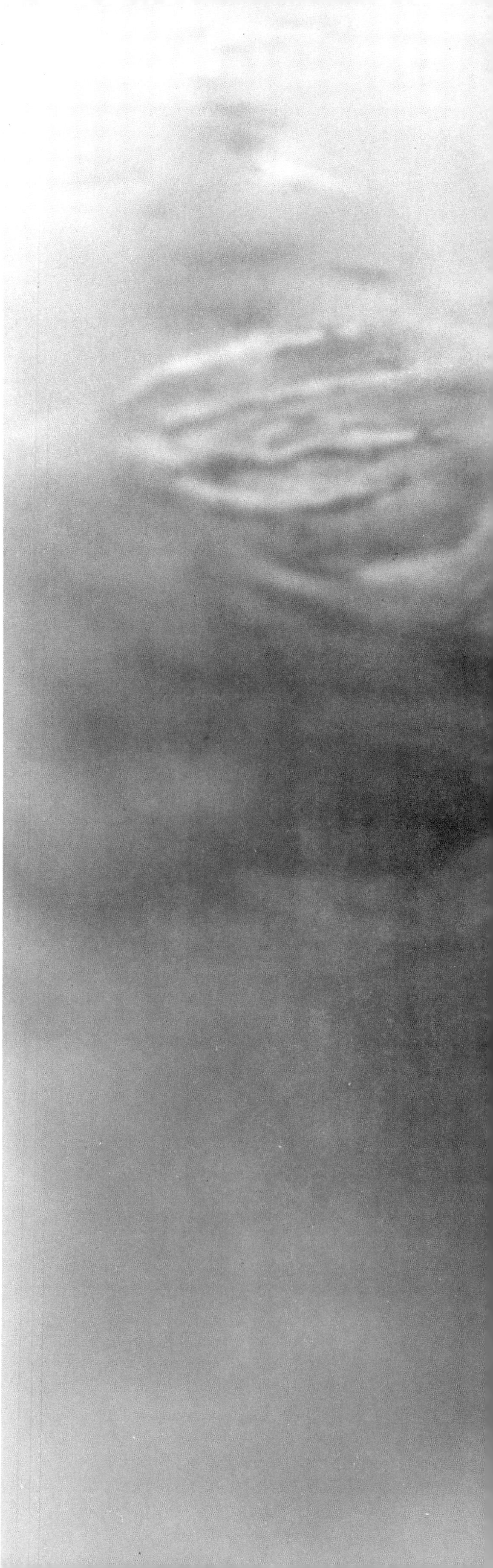

A dim, green light filtered through the leaves. Not a bird sang, and no breeze stirred the heavy vines. There was nothing to harm Lona and nothing to help her. Wrapped in her cloak, she slept on the hard ground. She drank from streams, and fed on berries. She wished a leaf would fall. She wished Rogain's voice would whisper from the jewel. The utter quiet was worse than facing dangers, but she went on.

She left the wood behind her, and in her way rose the savage mountains that guarded the three kingdoms. Their immense heights were enough to dizzy even a full-sized princess, but Rogain's jewel glowed steadily, and steadily small Lona toiled up and up. On the hillsides she met her first living creatures. Squirrels played around her, a shy deer drank from the same pool that quenched her thirst, and a rabbit shared its hole with her when a swooping eagle chased them both. Lona tried to talk to them as she always had to Toad, but these were true animals, and they spoke no human tongue.

By faith, and courage, and the magic of the jewel, Lona won safely over the mountains, and came at last to the shore of a grey sea.

It was a wild coast rimmed with rocks, and Lona climbed upon the tallest to scan an empty ocean. As she slid to earth again the solid stone beneath her quivered and became a monstrous dog. On every side the rocks were changing into beasts, as Druth's magic reached for her across the mountains.

One monster snarled at her, "Go back, go back! There is no way for you across the sea."

Another, smiling slyly, whispered, "Go back, foolish princess. You'll drown in that grey sea, and be washed up on a lonely shore with seaweed in your yellow hair. Go back to your safe castle."

How Lona longed to follow their advice! She trembled and half turned to flee, but the jewel's voice spoke quietly in her ear, "Don't heed them, Lona. There is no way for you except across the sea. Go forward."

Obediently Lona followed the jewel's light forward until the waves breaking over her feet stopped her. What was she to do now? All the long day she sat at the edge of the beach and waited for a sign.

The beasts behind her turned back to rocks, and back to beasts, and back to rocks, and howled their threats.

Lona kept her fingers in her ears, and her eyes on the endless water where no ships sailed and nothing changed but the ebbing tide. When the sun began to sink she sighed, lifted her skirts, and walked straight into the cold sea.

Suddenly, as the water closed around her, a voice called her name, and a boat drifted toward her. It was nothing but a raft half awash with the waves, manned by a grey goose made of wood.

"Climb aboard, Princess Lona," said the goose. "I loved a princess once. I was a goodly knight then, and she was as fair as you. We crossed the path of the Wizard Druth, and he had a mind to change my princess into a grey goose. When he failed with her, his anger turned on me. So while Druth's power lasts I live trapped inside this wooden body. But I know of the magic shell you seek, and I can take you safely over the sea."

Lona trusted the enchanted goose. She slept securely the night through while the goose kept watch, and the raft floated softly over a calm ocean. When morning broke there was a wisp of land on the horizon. It grew to an island lying low in the water, and before the sun was high the wooden goose set Lona ashore where grey driftwood tangles met the pale sand.

"Cross the island," he told her, "and climb the great dunes. Seek your shell on the beach beyond."

"I thank you, brave goose," said Lona.

"I wish you well," replied the goose, and he was gone.

The island was a place of sky, and sand, and wind, where nothing grew but the harsh sea grasses. The sand filled Lona's eyes and trapped her feet. The wind snatched her up and flung her down until she was battered and breathless. Each time it was harder to struggle up again. Lona thought how easy it would be just to lie there until the shifting sand covered her and she was safe from the wind forever.

"There's no safety under the sand, Lona," came a cry from the jewel. "You must go forward."

"I can't," thought Lona, but she struggled on.

The wind fought her every step up the dunes, but as she came over the crest it eased to a breeze that nudged her down the other slope to a wide beach strewn with a bewilderment of shells. It dropped to a breath that barely stirred her curls as she ran among the shells, touching one, listening to another.

It died entirely as a hand rose out of the sand and offered Lona a a shell that sang a song of all the waters in the world. Lona took the shell in her arms, and in the great quiet that the wind had left the shell spoke:

"When the Wizard's power is broken
By the words that I have spoken,
Let the waters over Muirlan
Vanish like an evil dream."

In far-off Muirlan the lake drained away. The people rose from their long enchantment. They dumped the fish from their cottages, and pulled the lily pads from their towers, and took up their lives again. There was much cautious glancing over shoulders and muttering of Druth's name, but Druth was too busy brewing spells for Lona to take heed of Muirlan's freedom.

On the island Lona stood cradling the shell. She felt it tug gently against her clasping arms, and let it go. It floated beside her, and from its rosy, polished curves came the song again. Lona never forgot that song. It made her see the surge of the sea in anger, the splash of little waves where children played, green valleys of water lifting to foam-flecked crests, and the twinkling feet of sandpipers. The notes of the song changed into the flutter of wings until a flock of great gulls was circling overhead. As the last note died the shell faded away, and Lona was left to the hovering birds.

A strong claw grasped her wrist, and a beat of wings lifted her high in the air. With the shell's song in her ears she was one with the birds, and she watched the earth curve beneath her without fear.

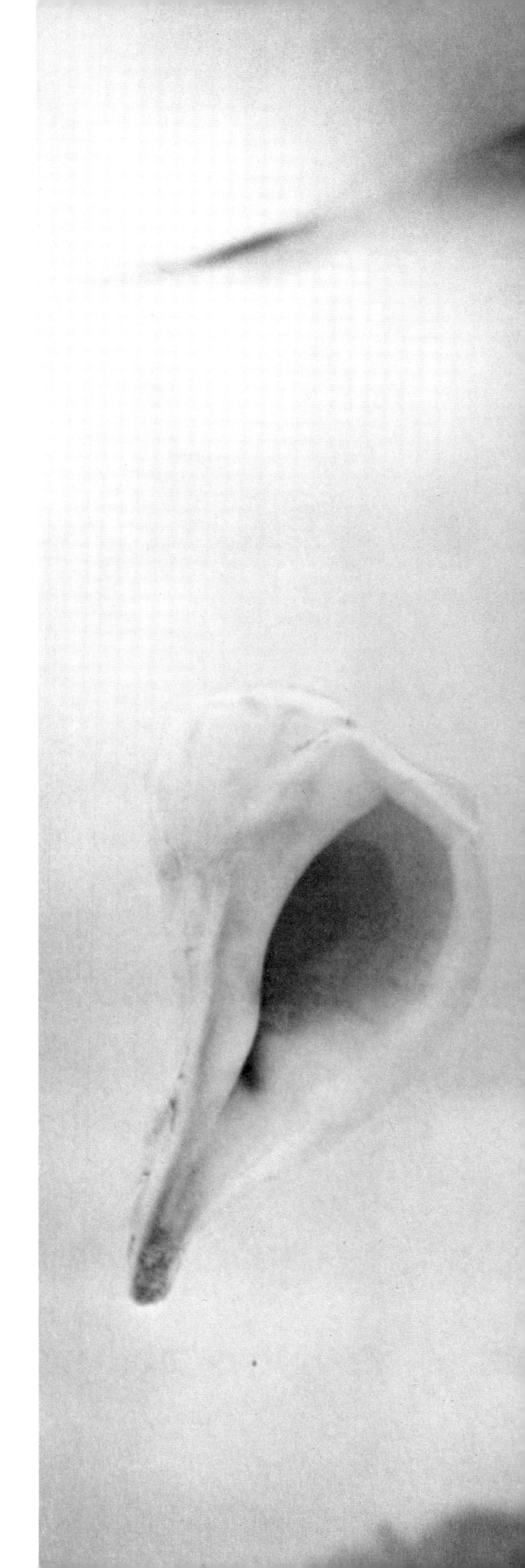

The gulls carried her far over the moving sea. Lona twisted her head to watch the color of the water changing below her. The clear turquoise of the southern seas, streaked with green and purple, softened into grey, then turned a strong, cold blue as the birds flew ever northward.

"How lovely to have wings," thought Lona.

Where a great headland jutted from the shore the gulls circled lower and lower, and dropped Lona on a rocky height.

The ground was warm under her shoulders. The slopes around were clothed in thyme and heather, and a veil of bees hummed over them. The warmth and the sweet smells and the humming filled Lona with a drowsy contentment. She had to shake herself awake. She sat up yawning, and reached in the pocket of her cloak for Rogain's jewel. It was gone!

Lona turned her pockets inside out. She searched the ground all around her, and grew frantic. Had she dropped the jewel in her flight? Did it lie now deep under the sea? "Oh, gulls, come back!" she screamed. "I need your help." But nothing moved in the uncaring landscape. Now she had no guide at all!

Lona felt as though she had lost Rogain himself.

The cliffs dropped sheer to the sea, and little wandering paths led this way and that. They were dimly worn as though by feet from long ago, and one looked like another. How was Lona to choose among them?

She picked one at random, and it ended abruptly at the edge of a chasm so deep that Lona dared not look over at the white foam curling on the rocks. She tried another, and it roamed round and round the headland and brought her back to where she had started. She chose a third. It led her straight inland until a shadow came between her and the sun. Lona looked up and saw a dark, enormous bird. Its shadow grew and reached, and enveloped her in a pool of cold, black shade. Lona stepped out into the sun, but the bird's shadow reached for her again. Step by step it drove her back to the cliff edge, while the bird croaked coaxingly. "Turn back, Lona. Give up. You are lost, and will never find what you seek. Trust me. I'll take you back to Yarmailt. Go home. Would you rather go over the cliff? Go home."

On the brink of the cliff Lona sank to her knees in the grass. Huddled there she wished desperately for the comfort of Rogain's jewel. But she knew very well what it would tell her. "Go forward, Lona." She crawled a little toward the bird. Its shadow grew less. As she advanced the shadow shrank. Suddenly the bird was gone with a cry, and Lona's way was clear.

But the way to where? Without her jewel one road was as good as another.

The days lengthened into weeks while Lona wandered on. One hot noontide, footsore and weary, she sank down by a still pool to rest and weep.

A white swan glided near, and wept with her.

"I know your trouble, and I share your grief," said the swan. "Once I was a queen, and had a daughter as fair as you. Druth the Wizard failed to put a spell on her, and soothed his anger by making me a swan. Now I fly from lake to lake, and add my tears to their waters. But I see many things, and I can help you. Not far from here you'll come upon a farm. There you will find an old, brown horse. Speak kindly to him, and follow where he leads."

"I thank you, royal swan," said Lona.

"I wish you well," said the swan, and she was gone.

Lona found the farm dozing in the sun. She crept to a window and saw a woman busy at her spinning. She poked her head inside an open door and smelled a stable for the first time—sweet hay, and manure, and the moist breath of the cows. But nowhere did she find an old, brown horse. In the farmyard there were only clucking chickens. Their feathered heads came as high as her waist, and their pecking bills drove her scurrying up a ladder out of their reach. At the top of the ladder she dug herself a warm, safe nest in the haystack, fell asleep there, and woke to the nudging of a velvety nose. She was looking into the kind eyes of a horse.

"Greetings, little princess," said the horse. "I served another princess once. She was as fair as you, and I was chief of all her councilors. Druth the Wizard tried a spell on her, and failed. It put him out of temper, and I was at hand. So now I am an old, brown horse working a farmer's fields. But I can still advise a princess. Come with me, and we'll seek news of your lost jewel."

Lona rode contentedly on the horse's broad back, glad to rest her small, tired feet. They traveled by quiet lanes, and talked together like old friends.

"There is a place I know where great birds nest—birds who scoop their living from the sea. We are going there," the horse told Lona. "The birds might have seen the glint of a jewel falling from the sky. They might have scooped more than fish from the sea."

"But if they had the jewel would they give it up to me?" wondered Lona, "Can I talk to them?"

"No, for they do not belong to the world of enchanted things. They cannot speak, nor have they any use for jewels. You can only try your luck."

When at last their journey ended Lona was sad at parting from her new friend.

"Stay with me," she begged.

"This is as far as I can take you, Princess Lona," the horse answered gently. "Listen! Don't you hear the birds? Go seek them."

He knelt to let Lona slide to the ground.

"I thank you, kind horse," said Lona.

"I wish you well," replied the horse, and he was gone.

The harsh bird cries guided Lona to a circle of huge, untidy nests upon the shore. Lona sat down in their midst, and tried by sign and voice to ask the clustering birds about her jewel. The birds could not understand, but they were kind. They welcomed Lona, and tried to please her. They brought their fledglings to see her, and filled her lap with fresh-caught fish.

"I'll never make them understand," thought Lona in despair, as she smoothed a fledgling's head and tried politely not to turn her head away from the slippery offering in her lap.

Then came a bird who carried something gleaming clamped in his beak.

It was Rogain's jewel, and he dropped it in her lap among the fish!

Unbelievingly Lona lifted the jewel and held it to her cheek. Her joy was so great that even the birds could see it. They flapped their wings in satisfaction at having pleased her at last with this bit of bright stone they had plucked by chance from the waters.

The jewel in Lona's hand was silent. She held it up and took a step northward. The jewel's glow dimmed. She turned to the east, and the jewel grew cloudier. She turned south, and found that she held a grey stone. She swung to the west, and light leaped from the jewel's glowing heart. So westward she went, with the birds speeding her on her way.

The jewel's light took Lona on and on. She saw strange peoples and wild lands. The rain wet her, and the sun dried her. She faced a thousand dangers. There were real perils to threaten her small, human form, and all Druth's phantom horrors to threaten her courageous heart. When she grew tired or frightened beyond bearing, the jewel would comfort her in Rogain's voice, and once again she would go forward.

The fine linen of her dress wore thin. Her red cloak faded to a dingy brown. Her bare feet were as tough as any peasant girl's. And always she was lonely. But she went on. The months grew into one year, then two, and started on a third. As the third year drew toward its close Lona was crossing a silent plain where yellow dust storms swirled. Beyond the silence and the storms she found a sunny wood of towering trees. She would have lingered in its peace, but the jewel led her straight to the mightiest tree of all, and would not let her turn away. The branches heaved in creaking turmoil, and, with a rending and a wrenching, a narrow split opened in the heart of the tree, and Lona passed through.

The sunlight was left behind her, and Lona entered a sad, cold world. She drew her cloak about her against the piercing wind, and stole cautiously along an aisle of bare tree trunks. There seemed to be no sky overhead, only the tree trunks reaching up into infinity. A horse's hoofs sounded in the distance, and Lona saw a far-off glimmer of armor. A mounted knight was riding toward her. Soon his great war horse loomed above her, and the knight's hand beckoned her to him. Lona would have obeyed, but a wall of fire sprang up between them! Through the flames the knight still beckoned. Again and again the heat drove Lona back. Every flame had a tongue that hissed Druth's warnings: "Go back. You'll not pass here. Try, and you'll be burned to black ashes. In Yarmailt your castle waits. There's safety there. Go back! Go back!"

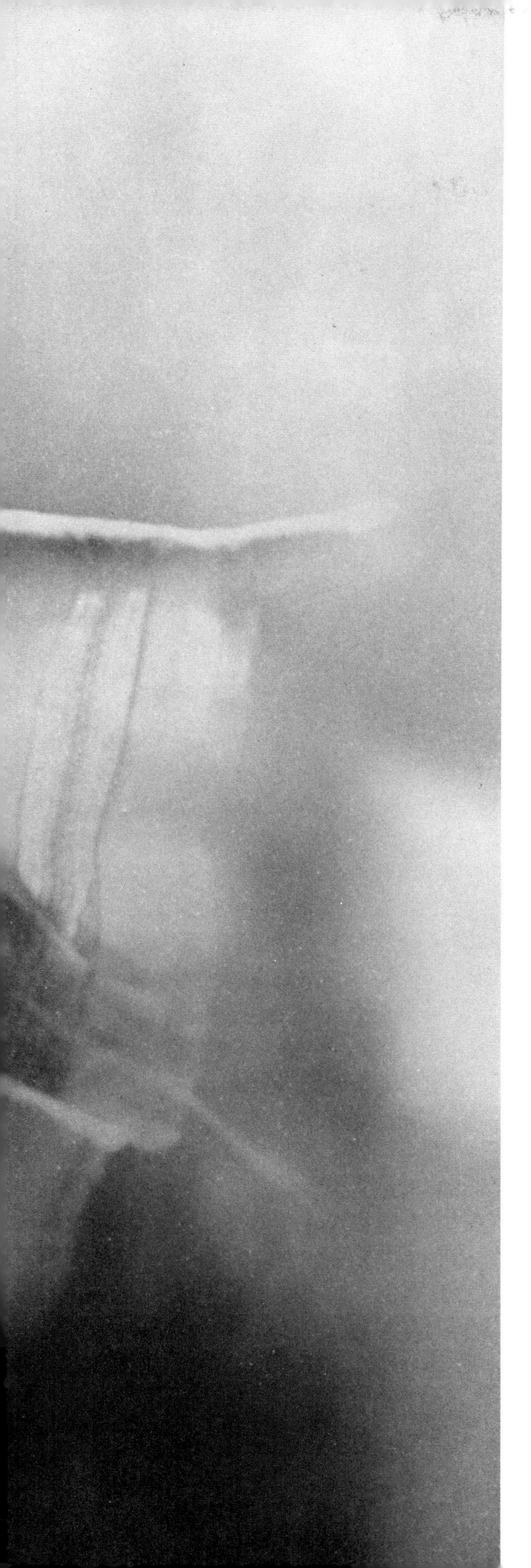

Lona ran up and down trying to outflank the fire, but it seemed to reach across the world. Still the knight beckoned, and a voice echoed from the jewel: "Go forward once again, Lona, if you would free Lasair."

So Lona shut her eyes, and leaped through the roaring flames. The heat struck her with the force of a heavy blow. The fire ran along the tendrils of her hair and scorched her skirts. Then she felt only a gentle warmth. She had won through, and stood at the knight's stirrup. He reached down a mailed hand, and lifted her to his saddlebow. He swung his horse around, and they were off like the wind, leaving Druth's raging fire far behind. The trees flashed past Lona's dizzied eyes, and the knight's hand bruised her small ribs, but she felt safe and protected in his grasp.

In a forlorn, bare glade the knight drew rein at last. Wordlessly he put a glowing key into Lona's fingers, and set her on the ground. She looked up to thank him, but he had already turned away into the forest, where he vanished like a mist.

Lona stood alone with the key warm in her hand.

"I hold Lasair's freedom," she murmured happily, and a voice from the key replied:

"When the Wizard's power is broken
By the words that I have spoken,
Let Lasair's long blackened ruins
Be swallowed in a tide of green."

Across the world in Lasair green shoots began to grow, and a trickle of water flowed again in the dry streams. The people woke from their long enchantment, and began to build anew in their blossoming land. Sweet-scented winds from Lasair drifted past Druth's dismal tower, but he never looked up nor sniffed the air.

In the barren glade around Lona the forest bloomed. Withered stalks straightened, and put out small flowers. Tightly curled ferns unrolled in the pale sunlight. It was suddenly spring in the woods.

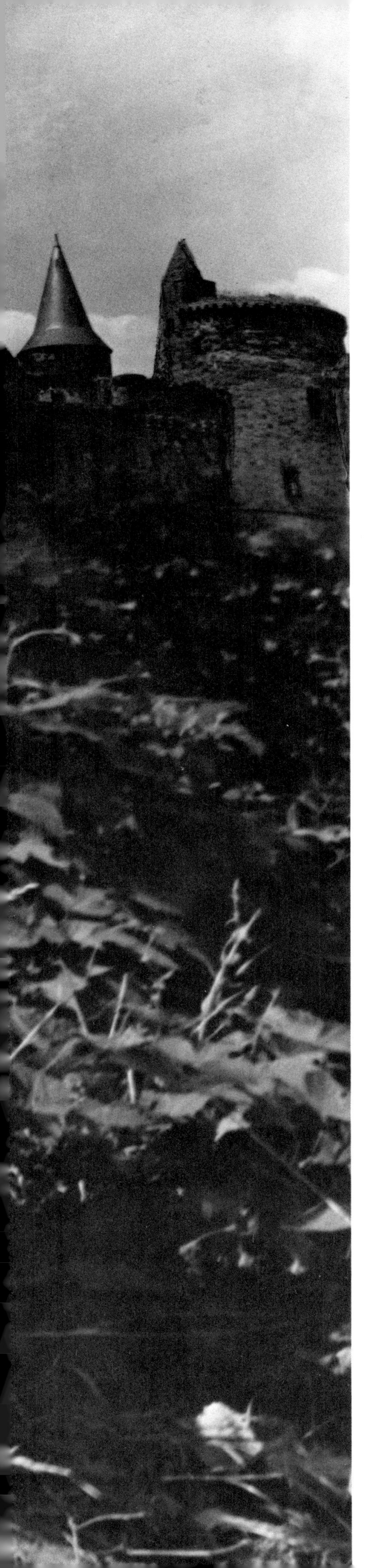

Then, before Lona could draw a deep breath, it was summer! A rush of pure joy swept over her. She swung the heavy key in her hand and scarcely noticed its weight.

Singing, she strolled out of the forest, feeling as safe as a princess in her own garden. When the towers of a splendid castle rose on the horizon and the jewel's light brightened, Lona felt that there she would find the end of all her seeking. Only summer fields lay between her and the moat that guarded it.

The drawbridge was down, its massive chains rusted beyond all use. As Lona set foot on the ancient planks the song died on her lips, and the soft air grew hot and dry and sullen. On the scrabbled earth before the castle was spread coil upon coil of a loathsome dragon. Two hideous heads stared down at Lona. Did she dare go forward? Was this Druth's dragon whom she could conquer by courage alone? The jewel still shone strong and bright. Shaking in every limb, Lona let its light draw her on until she stood under the arches of the monstrous necks.

The dragon reached out an immense claw and set it on the trailing end of Lona's cloak. The heads twisted toward her, and long tongues flicked her up and down.

"She tastes delicious," roared one head. "I think I shall eat her at once!"

"You ate the last princess," said the other head. "This one is mine. Of course she's very small. Barely a good mouthful. I might spare her if she hurried home and stayed where she belongs. Be sensible, little princess. Run away quickly to your own castle before it's too late."

"I mean to eat her now," hissed the first head, snapping at its brother.

In a minute a battle was raging above Lona. Flame and smoke filled the air while the greedy heads quarreled.

Lona dragged her cloak free, and ran for the castle gate!

She had just slipped through when the dragon hurled himself after her. The whole castle shook with the impact, but neither head could get through the gate. Two barbed tongues came licking in, seeking Lona blindly. With her eyes glued fearfully to the tongues she backed away. Pressed against the farthest wall she was just beyond their reach. About her stretched a vast, grass-grown courtyard. Stone shields around the walls bore coats of arms worn dim by time and weather. Dark doorways yawned on every side, and a flight of crumbling steps went upward. The steps led away from the dragon and the gate so wearily Lona started to climb them.

Rogain's jewel began to glow like a star!

The sight lifted Lona's heart and quickened her feet.

Above the steps there was a timeworn tower, and in the tower an almost hidden door. It was many a long year since anyone had passed this way, for the door was blocked by brambles and sealed with vines.

Lona's key slid easily into the rusted lock, but not all her strength could turn it. Then the key turned of itself, and with a tearing of branches the old door swung wide. Lona peered from the threshold to see what new danger awaited her in the chamber beyond. But there was no chamber beyond the door! There was only windy, star-filled space.

Lona hesitated before that tremendous void, but Rogain's voice called out triumphantly from the blazing jewel, "Go forward, Lona." Trustingly she stepped off the threshold.

The winds bore her up, and out of the stars whirled a golden crown. A voice from the crown sang out:

"When the Wizard's power is broken
By the words that I have spoken,
Let the fog that smothers Yarmailt
Melt into a sunlit day."

The crown came to rest on Lona's head, and she began to grow tall again. As she grew tall she grew thin as air, and vanished on the winds.

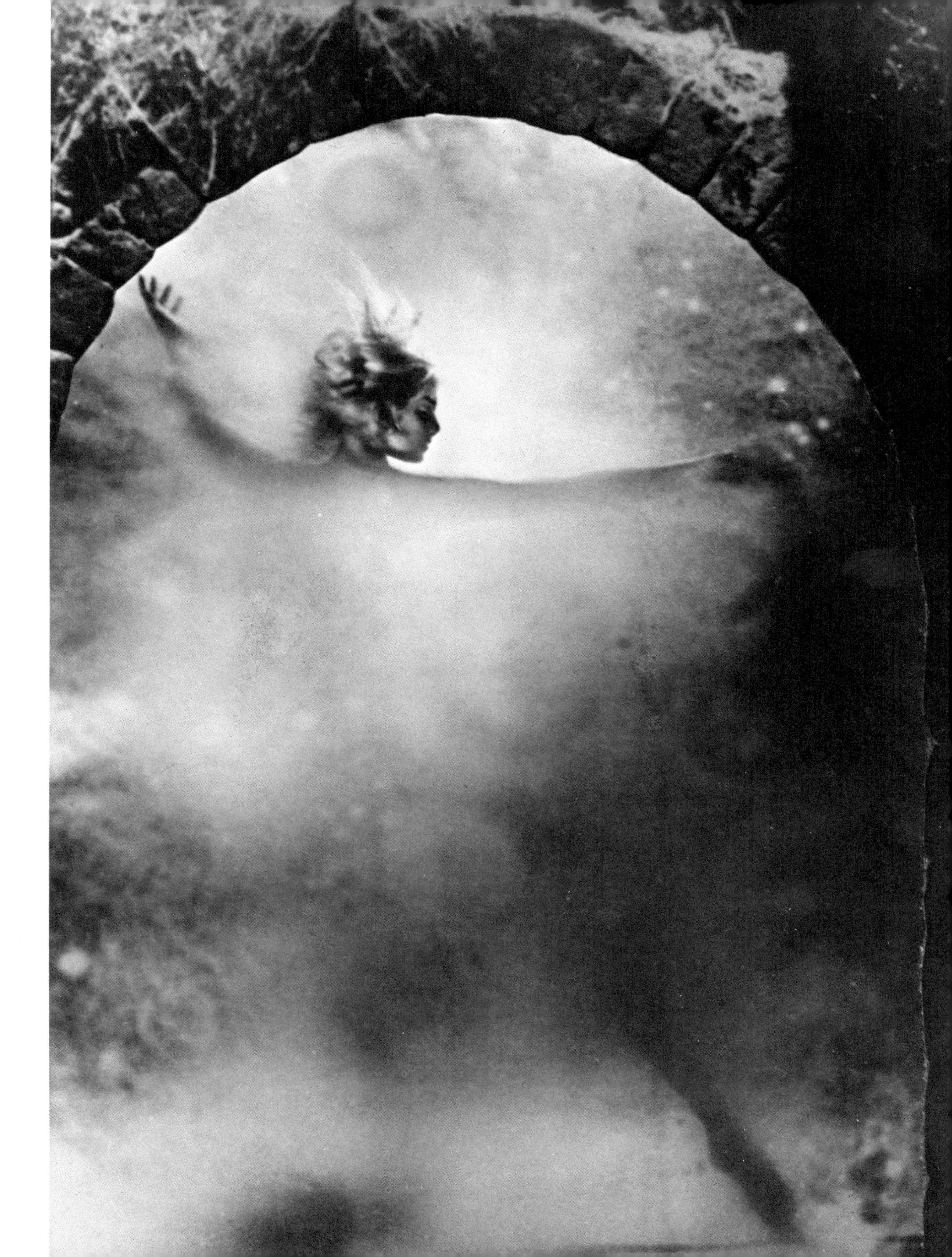

All Lona felt was a rush of air on her closed eyes, and when she opened them she was standing in her own castle, in her own turret room. There was a deep film of dust on everything. The dress that she had stepped out of so long ago still lay on the floor. Lona leaned down to pick it up, and realized then that she had regained her own true size. But had Yarmailt been restored as yet? She raced to the window. Faint mountains were emerging from the fog, and faintly in the distance Lona heard a hop and a plop on the stairs.

"Rogain!" cried Lona, and quicker than light she was into her dress, and running down the steps.

Had Rogain been here all the time awaiting her return, wondered Lona, or was it spring in Yarmailt and the time for his yearly visit? Her head was too muddled by magic for her to know what the season ought to be!

"I'd like it to be spring," she thought as she ran. "It would be lovely to see Yarmailt for the first time in the spring."

In the courtyard Rogain squatted, and Lona dropped to her knees beside him.

"Rogain, Rogain," she cried, "I have come home at last. Have I done well? Are the kingdoms saved? I have missed you so. Without your voice to speak to me from the jewel I would have failed a hundred times. Now that my task is finished, you must have your jewel again."

As she spoke Lona set the jewel back in Rogain's head.

And Rogain the Toad grew larger and larger, and dimmer and dimmer, and in a moment a tall prince stood in his place.

Lona turned away. This was not her Rogain the Toad! But Rogain's jewel shone on the strange prince's breast, and Rogain's voice came from his lips.

"I was a prince before I was a toad, a prince of Muirlan before I angered Druth," Rogain told her. "Do you like me less as a prince, Lona? I am no different in my heart."

Lona turned back, and looked long at Rogain.

"You are no different in my heart," she said at last.

She put her hands in his, and together they went down into the thinning fog.

Through great rents in the mist the fields and towns of Yarmailt were appearing.

"Behold, Lona, how your courage has defeated Druth," said Rogain.

"And now I must call three times upon his name, and let him change me as he chooses," said Lona. "Give me your hand again, Rogain."

"Stay silent, I entreat you," begged Rogain wildly.

But Lona knew that she must speak. Only if she did would the kingdoms stay safe forever. Only if she accepted Druth's spell would all his other spells be set at naught. Only if she were enchanted would the grey goose, and the white swan, and the kind, brown horse regain their own forms.

Holding tight to Rogain's hand, she whispered, "Druth, Druth, Druth——"

The words hung in the air as if reluctant at their errand, but in his distant tower Druth started to his feet. Lona was back in her castle, and his ultimate spell was ready. This time he would enchant a princess! He was sure of it. What should he make Lona—bird or beast, fish or reptile? What was uglier than a toad? Let her be a toad!

Druth's centuries of waiting were done at last. Rogain felt Lona's hand shrink in his. Before his eyes she dwindled into a small, brown toad. He lifted her tenderly, and set her on his palm.

"Toad or princess, I love you," Rogain told her, "but somewhere in the world there must be a spell to set you free, and we will find it."

"Prince or toad, I love you," said Lona, and together they set out on the long journey to learn the magic that would disenchant a princess.

The seasons turned.

Druth lay dead under the stones of his fallen tower.

The three kingdoms flourished, and every day their people, from the lowliest scullion to the proudest lord, thought gratefully of Lona and Rogain, and wished them well and a safe return.

There is great power in wishing. One day, hand in hand, home to their kingdoms came Lona and Rogain.

DARE WRIGHT

A gifted writer, with six previously published books to her credit—including the LONELY DOLL books and DATE WITH LONDON—she spent many months in perfecting a story that would meet her own high standards. Finding the right castles and other "props" for the pictures took a long time too, and Miss Wright's search led her to Scotland, the coast of Brittany, and even to Sicily.

Then came long hours spent in the darkroom of her studio in New York City, where employing her talents as a professional photographer, she carefully developed the many hundreds of photographs she had taken and, by careful pruning and skillful blending, produced the sequence of pictures that complement her text so effectively. That LONA is an artistic triumph will be apparent at once to those of discriminating taste.